JOY HOPE

LOVE FAITH

In the Nick of Time

Written by **Deedee Cummings**

Illustrated by **Charlene Mosley**

Interior Image Credit: Charlene Mosley

ISBN: 978-1-9512-1820-1 (sc)
ISBN: 978-1-9512-1822-5 (hc)
ISBN: 978-1-9512-1821-8 (e)

Lulu Publishing Services rev. date: 02/12/2020

makeawaymedia.com
deedeecummings.com

@makeawaymedia
@authordeedeecummings

Praise for In the Nick of Time

"Nick's transformation from a child concerned with material things to a kid who wants to help others rings true.... Mosley's textured cartoon illustrations, which feature painterly backgrounds, ground the story beautifully.... This engaging holiday tale gives children-like the protagonist-a chance to investigate their own privilege."
-KIRKUS REVIEWS

"It's about a boy who saves Christmas - a common enough storyline - but this one is different. After years of collecting children's Christmas books, Deedee Cummings couldn't find (this specific storyline) with a character who looked like her son. She knew how important it was for her son to see a character he could admire.
So she wrote her own."
-USA TODAY

"We all know and understand the importance of seeing oneself in the imagery we're exposed to on a daily basis from the very beginning. As children, we're sponges that inhale information and believe what we're told about ourselves. One way to mold the narrative your children subscribe to is with uplifting, inspiring books that feature faces that look like their own as protagonists."
-ESSENCE

Other books by the author:

Love Is...
Think of it Like This!
My Trip to the Beach
I Want to be a Bennett Belle
My Dad's Job
Heart
Kayla: A Modern—Day Princess
If A Caterpillar Can Fly, Why Can't I?
Like Rainwater
This is the Earth

This book is dedicated to my son Nick, who from birth has been the most funny, kind and considerate soul I have ever met. I wrote this book for you and so many little brown boys like you who do not see themselves very often in books, but especially in holiday books and stories. I longed for a story like this at Christmas time where you could feel like the hero, like the leader in kindness, and like someone that Santa could trust to call on for help. You can save Christmas (and the world) too.

"I like this book because it makes me feel like Christmas. And I like feeling like Christmas."

~10-year-old Nick

In the Nick of Time

"Nick! For heaven's sake, will you please keep it down? I mean really. The yelling is ridiculous." Nick's mom pokes her head around the corner.

"Sorry Mom. You know I can't control myself on this game."

"You will control yourself or you will not play it."

"Okay, okay, okay. I hear you."

Ding dong.

That's the doorbell. Nick wanted to yell for his mom, but he was afraid he'd get in trouble again. He stuck his head through the curtain on the side of the door. It was the mailman.

With a near blizzard outside Nick almost got blown away by sticking half of his body out the door to pick up the bag left behind.

He dragged the bag inside to the rug and dumped it out hoping the new game he ordered had arrived.

Nick sifted through the contents.

Letter for Mom. Letter for Dad.
Letter for Mom. Box for Dad.
Box for Mom.
Letter for... wait a minute.

I think this letter is for Santa!

Nick threw on his coat and boots and tried to catch the mailman, but he was lost in the snow.

"Stupid mailman!"

Nick plopped the mail down on the counter.

"What did you just say?" Nick's mom was back.

"I said **stupid mailman** Mom! Look at what he left."

"I don't care what he did. You don't call people stupid Nick. Ever. That is the second time I've heard you say that today and I do not want to hear it again."

"Mom, look, the mailman delivered this letter addressed to Saint Nick and I still didn't get my new game I ordered."

"Accidents happen. That makes them— accidents, not the people who made them— stupid. It's obviously an error. Your name is Nick Saint."

"Waste of my time!" Nick said.

"Oh really? Well I'll tell you what. We are going to open this letter Mr. waste-of-my-time."

"You cannot be serious." Nick was in disbelief.

"I could not be more serious. Have a seat."

Nick's mom patted the seat next to her and Nick sat down.

Together they opened the letter to Saint Nick.

Dear Saint Nick,

I hope this letter makes it to you before Christmas. My family lost our home. We have nowhere to live. My mom ~~sais sayss~~ says we can't get a place to live until she has a job. My Christmas wish is for my mom to get a job. Maybe my brother can have a truck if it is not too late to ask. A friend told me you are not real, but my mom said you are, if you believe. I believe.

Cooper E.

"He wrote a letter to Santa and he asked for a job for his mom? **That is so sss...**"

"**You better not say it.**" Nick's mom interrupted him before he could get himself into more trouble.

"Come on mom! Santa has a toy factory. Not a job factory." Nick explained.

"Nick Saint, what a privileged life you lead to not understand why someone would ask for something like this. There is nothing stupid about it."

"I once heard my school principal tell a teacher that it was stupid to ask for things you know won't happen." Nick shrugged his shoulders.

"I don't care who says it, it does not make it right. There is nothing stupid about people asking for what they need."

"Hmm... Cooper E.?
I think he goes to my school."
Nick thought out loud.

"Then Nick Saint, this is your lucky day."

"Mom, I can't do anything about a
grown-up needing a job."

"You can do more than you know.
You just have to try.
Think about it."

Nick found out that the Cooper E. who attends his school and the Cooper E. who wrote the letter were, in fact, the same person. He wrapped up one of his favorite video games and left it in Cooper's locker when no one was looking.

When Nick saw Cooper he asked,
"I heard you got a new video game! Did you like it?"

Cooper said that he loved the video game but,
"Unfortunately I can't play it. I don't have an Xbox."

Nick was thrown for a loop. Who doesn't have an Xbox? He thought.

Cooper added that it really wouldn't matter if he had an Xbox. "My family lives in a shelter. We only have one room with two outlets. We have a lot of stuff that needs to be plugged up before an Xbox. I wouldn't be able to play the game anyway."

Never did it cross Nick's mind that every child in his school did not have a home or even, video games to play. He had never heard of this.

No one ever talked about this. It wasn't on any TV shows he watched. Everyone he knew had a home, or so Nick thought. He asked Cooper to tell him what living in a shelter was like for him and his family.

Cooper told him that there are a lot of nice people who live there. A lot of families just like his, but this place was not home. Cooper said, "I just wish we had our own home again and that my brother could have a truck."

Wow, Nick thought.
With all that Cooper does not have, and with all that Cooper could have asked for, the things that Cooper wanted most were not even for himself.

Cooper's Christmas wishes were for those he loved the most.

Nick could not stop thinking about what he heard.
What if I tried to answer this letter for Santa?
After all, there is no way it can get to Santa in time.

Nick went home that night and told his mom all that he had learned. Now, for the first time in Nick's life, he too wanted something for someone else. He wanted Cooper's mom to find a job, so that his brother could have room to play with his truck, and the family could have a home with outlets in every room.

Hopefully, there'd be one outlet left for Cooper to have his own video game system. Nick wanted to do something, but he was just a kid, what could he do? And how? One thing was for sure- it had to happen before Christmas, but Nick didn't know where to start.

Nick's mom rubbed his back and said, "I am so proud of you son. You figured it out."

"I did?"

"You did."

Nick and his parents busily began working on their idea.
There wasn't much time left until Christmas Day.

With the school's help they were able to coordinate a job fair and a toy drive for all the families in need at their school. Nick was surprised to learn how many families needed help with things like food and winter coats, and help finding a place to work. He always thought you would be able to tell by looking at someone that they needed help, but he learned this was not true.

Cooper's mom was hired on the spot by Nick's family's company. She also picked up a big bag of toys to give to her boys, including the truck and video game system Nick personally helped find for his new friend and his friend's little brother.

Nick went to sleep that night feeling so grateful for everything he has, but mostly he felt grateful for the ability to help others. Nick would not see Christmas the same ever again.

The next day Nick greeted the mail carrier at the door with a cup of hot cocoa. She graciously accepted the cup and handed Nick the mail with a warm smile.

At first Nick thought that the mail carrier had made a mistake and delivered the wrong envelope again, but with a closer look, Nick read that this letter said:

To: Nick Saint
From: Saint Nick

Nick's eyes were as wide as two game controllers! He sat back on the couch looking all around him. *Can he see me?* Nick wondered about Santa's watchful eye.

Nick opened the letter.

Dear Nick,
I hear we share some of the same things.
Our name for one, a big heart for two,
and the joy that Christmas brings.
Some people seem to think
that Christmas
is all about what you can get.
But you and I know that this season means
to give, to hope, and to love without regret.
Congratulations young man you figured it out.
Your friendships and your future shine.
Don't forget the lesson you learned
when I needed you most—
And you were just in the nick of time.

Love always,
St. Nick